For my parents

my children

my husband

and two hamsters!

British Library Cataloguing in Publication Data
A catalogue record for this book is available from the British Library

ISBN 0 340 67258 7 Hardback
ISBN 0 340 67259 5 Paperback

Text and illustrations copyright © Deborah Inkpen 1998

The right of Deborah Inkpen to be identified as the author of this work
has been asserted by her in accordance with the
Copyright, Design and Patents Act 1988

10 9 8 7 6 5 4 3 2 1

First published 1998
by Hodder Children's Books,
a division of Hodder Headline plc,
338 Euston Road, London NW1 3BH

Printed in Hong Kong by Wing King Tong

HARRIET

DEBORAH INKPEN

Hodder
Children's
Books

A division of Hodder Headline plc

Harriet had escaped. Her cage was old. Some of the bars were bent.

She had gnawed at them with her teeth, pushed at them with her paws and eventually they had moved, just enough.

And now she was free.

Before her lay a huge carpet of green. Above her giant plants spread their leafy fingers. And over them all stretched the blue sky.

Harriet's whiskers quivered. Her nose twitched. The air was full of new sounds and new smells.

She scampered along the garden path nosing this way and that.

A dark shadow passed above her. Harriet scurried for cover. The shadow flew into a tree and started to sing.

A rich earthy scent led Harriet into the vegetable patch. She nibbled a spiky leaf. It tasted strange.

Then she nibbled some lettuce. That tasted good.

The carrots and the cabbages were good too.

But she didn't like the slugs. They were horrible.

Harriet paused to sniff the air. A weedy, watery smell made her feel thirsty.

She followed the smell to the edge of a murky pond.

As she leaned over to drink, a big warty toad popped up its head.

Harriet jumped! And went plummeting into the pond.

Plop!

The little hamster bobbed to the
surface like a cork.

The water was cold and full of green,
slimy weed that clung to her fur.

Gasping and spluttering, she paddled
to the edge and scrambled out,

a tiny,

soggy,

cross heap of fur.

The tiny heap of fur shook itself, smoothed down its coat, cleaned its whiskers and turned back into a little Russian hamster.

Harriet yawned sleepily.

'Here's a good place to sleep,' thought Harriet. Under the apple tree were lots of small holes. Something disappeared into one of them.

She peered down the hole.
A small face looked out.
It fixed Harriet with
black, beady eyes.

'You can't come here,' said a little grey mouse. 'Only mice live here.'

'You're not a mouse,' said another. 'You haven't got a tail.'

'What are you?' said a third.

Harriet told them that she was a Russian hamster and that she did have a tail. She turned around to show them. They seemed unimpressed.

'There's no room for hamsters here,' they said. 'Only mice.' And they vanished down their hole.

H arriet tried sleeping inside a flower pot,
but cobwebs stuck to her whiskers.

The watering can made
scary, echoing noises.

And a funny old glove looked
inviting, but smelled disgusting.

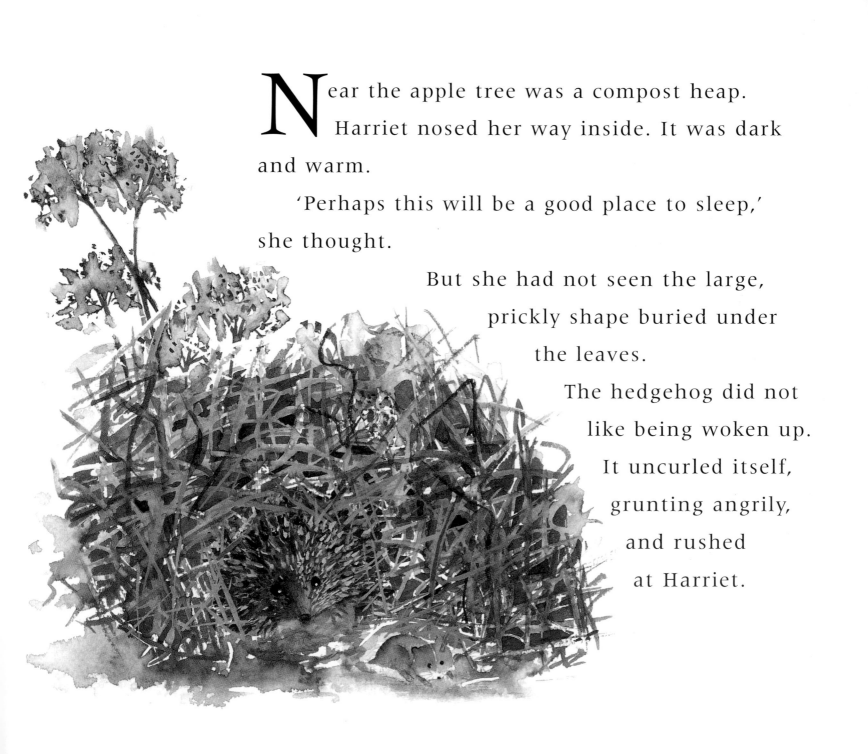

ear the apple tree was a compost heap.
Harriet nosed her way inside. It was dark and warm.

'Perhaps this will be a good place to sleep,' she thought.

But she had not seen the large, prickly shape buried under the leaves.

The hedgehog did not like being woken up. It uncurled itself, grunting angrily, and rushed at Harriet.

Harriet ran across the open lawn, tripping and rolling and running again. Some wire netting blocked her path. She pushed her nose underneath and wriggled through.

Scrambling up the side of a low wooden shed, she found herself on the roof. She scampered this way and that, looking for a place to hide.

Under the eaves was a dark hole. Harriet scrambled through and tumbled into darkness.

Squawk! A huge, foolish-faced creature flapped its wings and rushed around the coop.

Harriet dived beneath a clutch of warm eggs and watched as hens scattered in every direction.

Gradually the noise died down. The air began to clear. A big, fat, feathery body plumped down on top of her.

She snuggled back feeling safe and warm. And at last she fell asleep.

Harriet did not wake when the hen left the nest. She did not wake when chubby fingers began to collect the eggs. Nor did she wake when a delighted voice squealed,

'There you are, Harriet!'

The sleepy little hamster was popped carefully into an egg basket.

'Come on then,' said the voice. 'Let's take you home.'

But Harriet did not hear. She did not even stir.